The SANDAL Artist

The SANDAL Artist

By Kathleen T. Pelley

Illustrated by Lois Rosio Sprague

PELICAN PUBLISHING COMPANY

Gretna 2012

*To Father Vince, who planted the seed of this story and shows us all
how to shine like the sun—K. T. P.*

*The word "Pelican" and the depiction of a pelican are
trademarks of Pelican Publishing Company, Inc., and are
registered in the U.S. Patent and Trademark Office.*

ISBN 9781589809109

Printed in Singapore
Published by Pelican Publishing Company, Inc.
1000 Burmaster Street, Gretna, Louisiana 70053

The Sandal Artist

Long ago in Italy, there lived a poor young artist called Roberto. Every day Roberto strolled through the cobbled streets of his village and watched the children playing. Sometimes, one of the children would call out, "Roberto! Come and paint our picture."

But Roberto only laughed. "No!" he said. "One day I am going to be a great artist, and I must practice painting only beautiful things—not ragged children." So the children went back to their games, and Roberto headed off into the countryside to paint lush, green meadows and cool, lavender forests.

Every evening as he trudged back to his cottage, Roberto passed Stefano and his donkey, Benito, pulling a cart heaped with firewood. Often Stefano would call out to him, "Roberto! Why do you never paint our picture? Don't we make a handsome pair?"

But Roberto only smiled as he gazed at Stefano's tattered shirt and his scrawny donkey. "I'm sorry, Stefano," he said. "I don't have time to paint your picture, for one day, I am going to be a great artist, and I must paint only bright and wonderful things." So Stefano and his donkey continued hauling their firewood, while Roberto returned to his cottage.

On Sundays and holy days, Roberto packed up his easel and paints and headed off into the city. Roberto often saw Anna, the beggar woman, sitting on the steps of the village church. "Roberto!" she would cry out. "Come and paint my picture! See how pretty I can smile for you."

But Roberto only shook his head as he saw her withered face crinkle into a toothless grin. "No, Anna," he said. "I've told you before. I want to be a great artist, and I must paint only that which is filled with grace and light." So Anna went back to her begging, and Roberto headed into the city. There, he painted the glistening spires of the cathedral and turtledoves splashing in fountains.

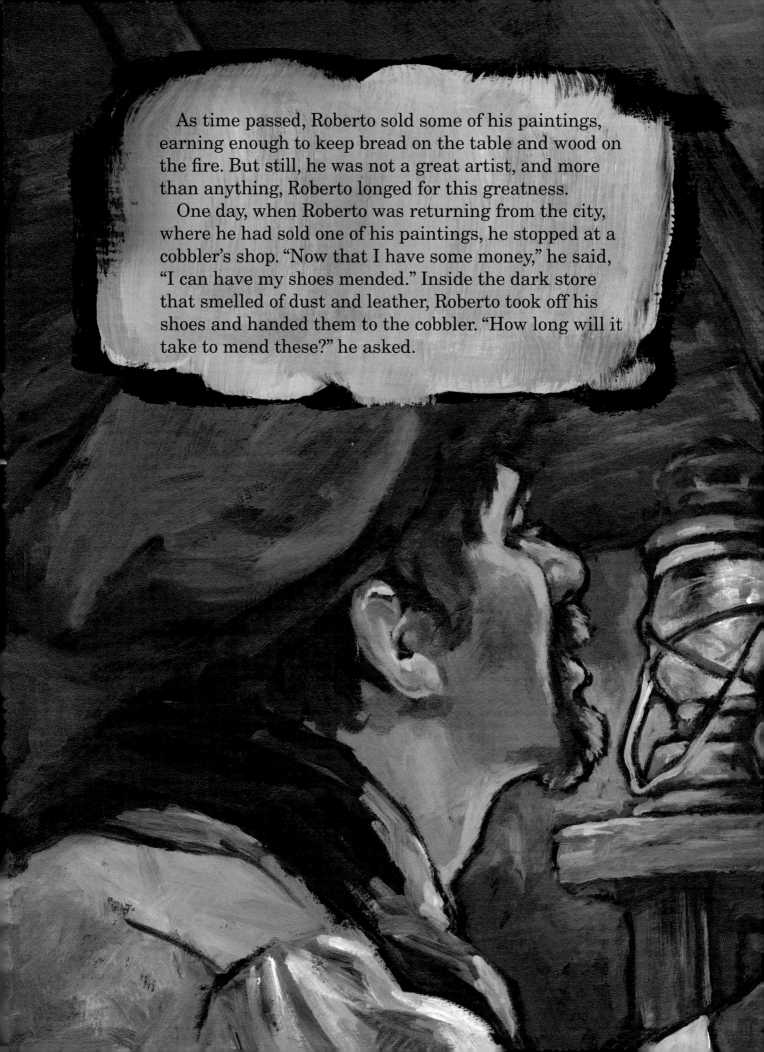

As time passed, Roberto sold some of his paintings, earning enough to keep bread on the table and wood on the fire. But still, he was not a great artist, and more than anything, Roberto longed for this greatness.

One day, when Roberto was returning from the city, where he had sold one of his paintings, he stopped at a cobbler's shop. "Now that I have some money," he said, "I can have my shoes mended." Inside the dark store that smelled of dust and leather, Roberto took off his shoes and handed them to the cobbler. "How long will it take to mend these?" he asked.

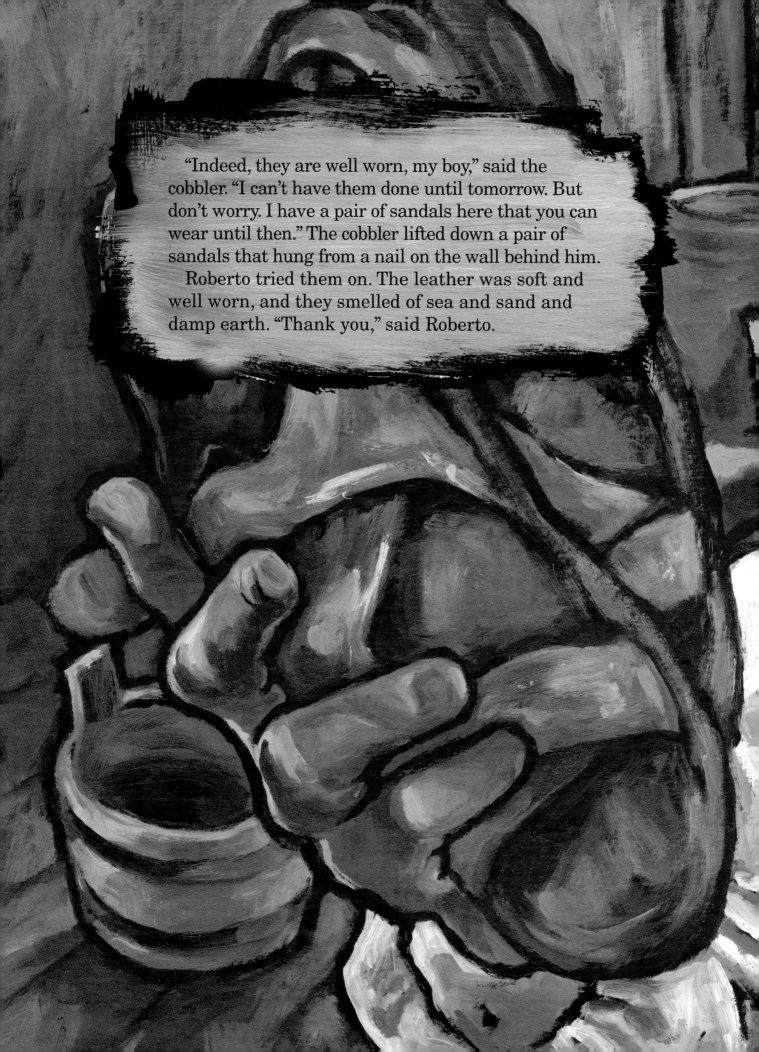

"Indeed, they are well worn, my boy," said the cobbler. "I can't have them done until tomorrow. But don't worry. I have a pair of sandals here that you can wear until then." The cobbler lifted down a pair of sandals that hung from a nail on the wall behind him.

Roberto tried them on. The leather was soft and well worn, and they smelled of sea and sand and damp earth. "Thank you," said Roberto.

But as Roberto turned to leave, the cobbler grabbed him by the arm and whispered, "There are some who say that if you wear another man's shoes, you will see the world with his eyes and feel it with his heart. So keep your eyes and heart open wide, my boy. Who knows what secrets you may find?"

Puzzled by the old man's words, Roberto stepped out into the street and headed for home.

When he arrived at his village, Roberto saw the children playing by the stream. One by one, they ran and leaped across the water, shrieking with delight. But standing alone beneath the willow tree was a little boy, who was lame. As the children's laughter grew louder, the boy's face crumpled with sadness.

Then an older boy came bounding up, scooped the child up in his arms, and hoisted him onto his shoulders, saying, "It's your turn now, Francesco!" And Roberto smiled as he saw little Francesco sitting there high and mighty, like a king on his throne.

"Tomorrow," said Roberto, "I will paint these beautiful creatures." Then he turned and went on his way.

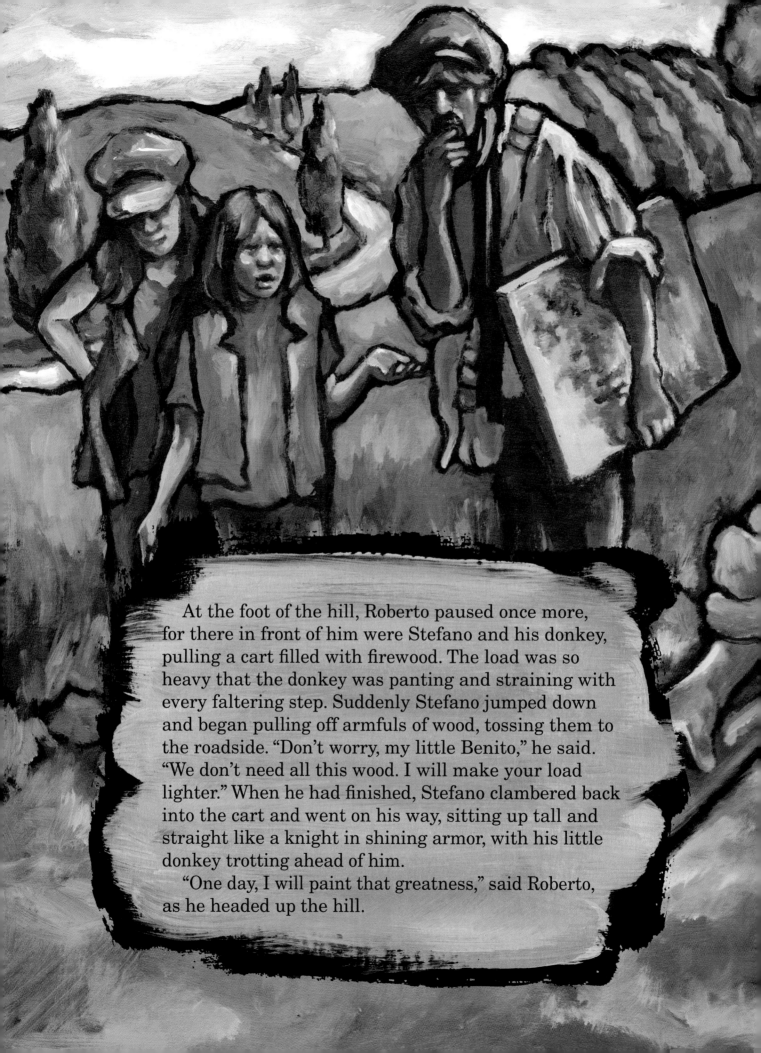

At the foot of the hill, Roberto paused once more, for there in front of him were Stefano and his donkey, pulling a cart filled with firewood. The load was so heavy that the donkey was panting and straining with every faltering step. Suddenly Stefano jumped down and began pulling off armfuls of wood, tossing them to the roadside. "Don't worry, my little Benito," he said. "We don't need all this wood. I will make your load lighter." When he had finished, Stefano clambered back into the cart and went on his way, sitting up tall and straight like a knight in shining armor, with his little donkey trotting ahead of him.

"One day, I will paint that greatness," said Roberto, as he headed up the hill.

Outside the church, Roberto stopped yet again. There in front of him, sitting on one of the gravestones, was Anna, the beggar woman. Her dress billowed around her as she stretched her arms out to her sides and cried, "Come, my beauties! Come to Anna!" A flock of sparrows swooped down and perched along her arms and shoulders.

There, in the shadowy twilight, Roberto watched the old woman's face light up in a glow of love. "One day," he whispered, "I will paint your grace and light." Then Roberto returned to his cottage and fell asleep.

In the morning, Roberto hurried into the city and burst into the cobbler's shop. "Tell me, I beg you," he cried, "whose shoes were these? What manner of man ever walked this earth and loved like this?"

The cobbler shook his head. "No one knows for certain, my boy. Long ago, a hermit gave these sandals to my grandfather. He found them in a cave, where they'd been swept up by the sea. Some say that they were the shoes of a fisherman. Others say that he was a carpenter. And still others say that he was a storyteller."

Roberto smiled as he handed the sandals back to the cobbler. Then he put on his own shoes and returned to his village.

From that day, Roberto loved and lived and painted as never before. In time, he did become a great artist. His paintings were hung in castles and galleries all over the land. People called him the Sandal Artist, for instead of writing his name in a corner of his paintings as other artists did, Roberto drew only a pair of sandals. They were the same sandals that still hung from a nail in a cobbler's shop, and the same sandals that had shown Roberto how to see that everyone he met was shining like the sun.

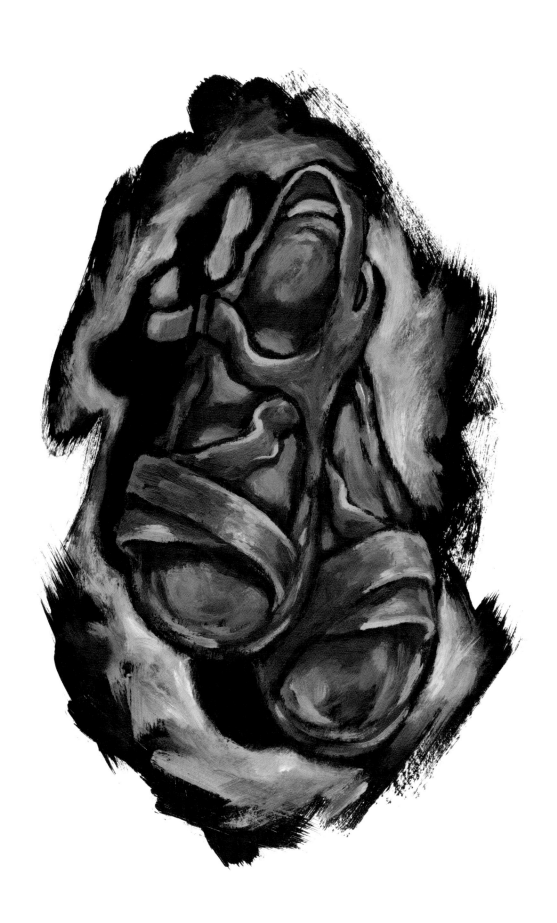